P9-CRQ-473

This Ladybird Book belongs to:

Jason Santanu Rayan

and mon

and you

This Ladybird retelling
by
Linda M Jennings

Ladybird books are widely available, but in case of
difficulty may be ordered by post or telephone from:

Ladybird Books – Cash Sales Department
Littlegate Road Paignton Devon TQ3 3BE
Telephone 0803 554761

A catalogue record for this book is available
from the British Library

Published by Ladybird Books Ltd Loughborough Leicestershire UK
Ladybird Books Inc Auburn Maine 04210 USA

Printed in EC

FAVOURITE TALES

Pinocchio

illustrated
by
PETER STEVENSON

based on the story by Carlo Collodi

Once there was an old woodcarver called Geppetto who longed to have a child of his own. So he decided to make a puppet that would be just like a real boy.

"I shall call him Pinocchio," said Geppetto as he began to carve the wood. A moment later, he had a surprise. As soon as Geppetto carved Pinocchio's mouth, the cheeky little puppet stuck out his tongue and laughed at him!

Geppetto's surprises were not over.
As he put the finishing touches to
Pinocchio, the puppet kicked the old
man on the nose and ran right
out of the door.

"Come back!" cried
Geppetto. But
Pinocchio ran on
down the street –
right into the arms
of a policeman!

Passers-by stopped and gathered around. "Let him go!" they pleaded. "That old man's a bully. He'll pull the puppet to pieces if he gets him back."

So the policeman let Pinocchio go and arrested Geppetto instead!

As soon as the old man had been taken away, Pinocchio returned home. Now he could do just as he liked!

As he lay down on the bed to rest, he heard a tiny voice nearby. "I'm the talking cricket," it said. "Be careful! Boys who don't listen to their fathers are always sorry later." But Pinocchio ignored the cricket.

After a while Pinocchio began to feel hungry, so he looked around for something to eat.

At last he found an egg. When he took it to the fire and tried to cook it, a little chicken popped out and flew away!

"I'll just stay here by the fire and keep warm," thought Pinocchio. Very soon the lazy puppet was fast asleep.

When Geppetto came home, he discovered that the fire had burned off the puppet's feet.

"Poor Pinocchio," said Geppetto sadly, giving him some pears to eat. "I'll make you some new feet, and I'll get you some clothes so that you can go to school like a real boy."

Geppetto was so poor that he had to sell his coat to buy Pinocchio a spelling book for school.

"Now off you go," he said, handing Pinocchio the book.

On his way to school, the
naughty little puppet heard some
music playing. "That sounds exciting,"
he thought. "I'll go and see where it's
coming from. It won't matter if I'm
late for school."

The music was coming from a travelling puppet show. The puppets invited Pinocchio to join them. "You'll soon be rich and famous!" they said.

The puppet master was angry at first, for the new puppet had almost stopped the show. But he soon forgave Pinocchio and let him dance and sing with all the other puppets.

Next morning the puppet master was much more friendly. He sent Pinocchio home with five gold coins to give to Geppetto.

As Pinocchio set off for home, he met a cat and a fox. The cat was pretending to be blind and the fox was pretending to be lame. Really, though, they were thieves.

The two wicked animals tried to steal Pinocchio's money, but he managed to run away. The thieves were so angry that they caught him and left him dangling from a tall oak tree.

Luckily, a beautiful blue fairy who lived nearby rescued Pinocchio and took him to her home.

The fairy knew that the puppet master had given Pinocchio some money, but when she asked Pinocchio about it, he said he had lost the coins.

As soon as he told this lie, Pinocchio's nose began to grow longer and longer. The fairy laughed. "That's what happens when you tell lies," she said.

Pinocchio was sorry he had been naughty again. "I wish I were a real boy," he told the fairy. "Can you help me to become one?"

"Yes," said the blue fairy with a smile, "but only if you are good and kind and brave." Then she told him how to get home to Geppetto.

Pinocchio hadn't got very far when he met the cat and the fox again. This time they *did* steal his money.

Pinocchio asked a policeman for help, but before he could explain what had happened, he found himself thrown into prison! To make matters worse, he heard that Geppetto was missing. The old man had gone to sea to look for Pinocchio, and his ship had been wrecked in a storm.

When Pinocchio was let out of prison, he really *meant* to go to school and be good. But he met some bad boys who persuaded him to run away.

Though he had fun at first, Pinocchio was soon in trouble again. In a place

called Toyland, he and the bad boys
were all turned into donkeys!

Pinocchio was put to work in a circus.
One day he hurt his leg and couldn't
work any more, so he was thrown into
the sea. As soon as he hit the water,
Pinocchio turned into a puppet again.
Then, as he drifted to the bottom, he
was swallowed by an enormous fish.

Pinocchio was amazed to find Geppetto inside the fish's belly, alive and well! This time Pinocchio wasn't naughty or lazy. Bravely, he led the kind old man to safety.

The blue fairy had been watching. "You deserve to have your wish, Pinocchio," she said. And to everyone's delight, she turned him into a real, live boy at last.